MAGICAL
FOLK TALES

Magical Folk Tales
ISBN: 978-93-5049-407-3

First Edition: 2013

© Shree Book Centre

Printed in India

Retold by
Sunita Pant Bansal

Published by

SHREE BOOK CENTRE
8, Kakad Industrial Estate, S. Keer Marg
Off L.J. Road, Matunga (W)
Mumbai - 400016 (India)
Tel : 91-22-24377516 / 24374559
Telefax: 91-22-24309183
E-mail: sales@shreebookcentre.com

CONTENTS

PREFACE

Ever wondered why the sun rises so early in the morning or why cats love to sit in the kitchen? We often take these things for granted. But everything around us has a story of how it came into being.

Folk tales illustrate a lesson, moral value, belief or custom that is considered extremely important by a particular folk culture. Initially passed down orally from one generation to another, these timeless tales give us a taste of our culture and tradition which differ from state to state. Some of these tales will make your child think, laugh, wonder, and will also help them in discovering hidden wisdom.

This book, a carefully-picked bouquet of six moral-based stories, has colourful illustrations. The simple language makes reading easier for your children, and the dialogue blurbs allow the characters to speak their mind. The meanings of difficult words at the end of the book will help your children to build their vocabulary.

The Fire Festival

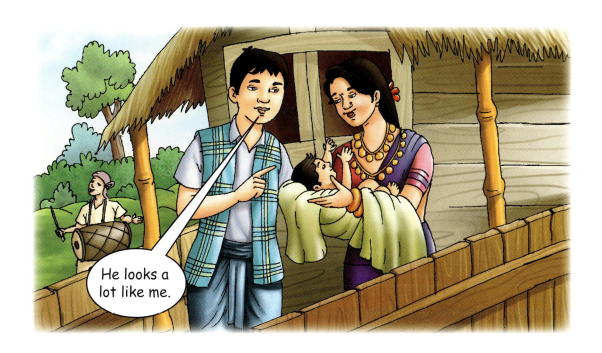

The folk tales from the state of Tripura are very popular among its people.

Long, long ago, the Chief of a tribal community had a son after many years. He was overjoyed at the birth of his son. He held a grand ceremony and other festivities

on the occasion. The Chief loved his son so much that he could not sleep if he was not near him at night!

One evening, the Chief sat under a big tree near his house. Some people of his tribe were also there. It was very warm and there was no rain. They could hear the tom-tom of the drums. Children of the tribe sang and danced near them.

"It has been a good year so far," the Chief said and the people clapped their hands. The tribal people always clapped their hands when they agreed with somebody or something. The Chief did not realise that his only son was not with him.

Then the Chief's wife came up to him and

It is time to put our son to sleep.

said, "Oh Chief, it is time for our son to sleep."

"Yes. But where is he? Isn't he with you in the house?" the Chief asked.

"Isn't he here, with you?" his wife asked, shocked.

The Chief stood up and said angrily, "Woman, I am telling you, he is not with me!

Go and look for him!"

"Oh, my dear Chief," the wife said anxiously. "He is not in our house."

The Chief then panicked and ordered, "Stop the dance! Let the drummers send out a message asking everyone to search for my son."

Immediately, the children stopped their

dance, and the drums began to talk. *"The Chief's child is lost,"* they said. *"Whoever finds the child must bring him to the Chief."*

All the people ran from place to place and looked for the boy.

But they could not find him. The Chief became extremely restless. He said, "All

my people must help me to find the boy. He is very precious to me."

Once again, the people from the tribe started searching for the Chief's son. They looked everywhere for the boy. The search for the boy went on for many hours.

Then all of a sudden a man cried out, "Chief! Here he is! Your son is here."

Father!

The Chief and his people ran up to the man. There, the boy was sleeping peacefully under a tree!

"Get up my dear," the Chief said anxiously to his little son. But the boy did not hear him.

"Get up," said his father again. The boy slowly opened his eyes.

"Father!" he said and got up. The Chief picked him up and hugged him. He was very happy to have his son back. However, he looked angrily at the tree.

"Burn that tree! It hid my son from me!" he said.

As the Chief's servants were about to put their torches on the tree's trunk and

branches, the Chief's son shouted, "Stop! Don't even touch the tree!"

The Chief was surprised. He said, "Son, let them burn the tree. I want to punish it."

The boy told his father, "Father, the tree did not hurt me. It protected me from the wind and the animals. Trees are our friends. We should not hurt them."

The Chief was ashamed. He said, "I am sorry. You are right. We will just burn the dry leaves and branches, but not the living trees."

From that day, the Chief announced the commencement of the Fire Festival. His people lit their torches and collected fallen leaves and branches. They started dancing

after putting their torches to the pile of leaves and branches.

Even now, the tribals care a lot about their environment and nature. They know that trees are precious for the survival of the earth.

Moral: Preserve our natural resources.

The Strangers And The Villagers

It seems to be a nice village.

The state of Punjab has many interesting folk tales that usually have hidden moral values.

A long time ago in Punjab, two travellers came to a small village in the evening. As they did not want to continue travelling at

night, they decided to stay at the village. They went to the house of the village Chief and asked, "Can we stay for the night in your village?"

"Of course, strangers! You are most welcome to stay here." said the Chief, "There is a rest house for travellers in our village. You may sleep there. And we will arrange supper for you. But remember one thing. There is an age-old custom in our village — strangers can sleep in the rest house, but they must not snore. We kill the person who snores!"

The two strangers went to the village rest house. They had a good supper and then they went to sleep. They slept quite well

for some hours. However, late in the night, one of them began to snore, "Zzzz, Zzzz, Zzzz."

The other stranger woke up when he heard his friend snoring. He sat up and thought, 'The people of the village will hear my friend snoring and kill him. I must do something to save him.'

The stranger thought of a plan and then broke into a warm smile. As his friend snored, he sang loudly:

Vo, Vo, Vo, Vo!

Vo, Vo, Vo, Vo!

We walked on the road.

We came to this village.

The people here were good to us.

Vo, Vo, Vo, Vo!

Vo, Vo, Vo, Vo!

He sang so loudly that the people did not hear his friend's snoring at all. Instead, they listened to the stranger's song and began to dance. A few of them even played drums and flutes along with the song. Some of them sang the song along with the stranger. Men, women and even the Chief sang and danced.

That entire night, one of the strangers sang and the other snored. All the people of the village sang and danced.

In the morning, the two strangers went to the Chief to bid goodbye and thank him for everything. The Chief gave them a small bag of money.

He said, "I am giving this money to both of you. We had a good time with you. We danced and sang well. Thank you very much for entertaining us the entire night."

The prize money made the two strangers very happy. They left the village to continue their journey. But, they started quarrelling for the Chief's money on the road. "How shall we divide the money?" asked one of them.

His friend said, "I must have three fourth of the money. You sang that song last night because I snored. So, I must get the major share."

The other stranger said, "Oh, is it so? The

villagers could have killed you because of your snoring. My song saved your life. You must actually thank me and give me the bigger part of the money."

They quarrelled for a long time, and yet could not decide anything.

A villager, who was passing by, overheard their argument. He said to them, "I see, you both have fooled us all. I will make sure that you two are punished severely."

The strangers got scared knowing their lives could be in danger. One of them pleaded to the villager, "Please, forgive us. You can take this money that we got from the Chief and let us go our way."

The villager agreed and took the bag. He

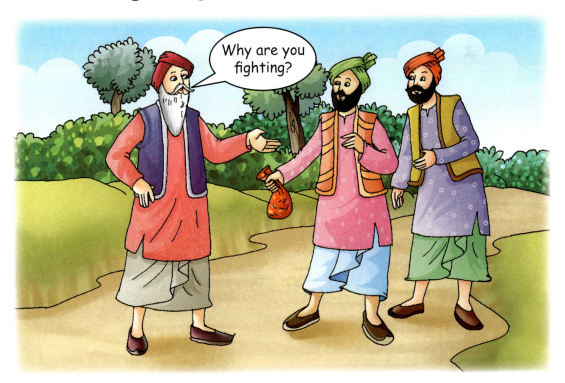

happily went back to the village with the money he got. The two strangers went on with their journey, empty-handed.

Moral: Foolish fights can benefit another person.

The Hawk, The Sun And The Cock

I need some money, dear friend.

The folk tales of Maharashtra are based on day-to-day incidents. One such story is that of the Sun and the Hawk.

A long time ago, the Sun said to the Hawk, "Dear friend, I need a favour from you. Will you please lend me some money? I

shall return it to you very soon."

The Hawk agreed to help the Sun and gave him some money. A month passed. But the Sun did not give back the money. Finally, the Hawk decided to go to the Sun and ask for his money. He went to the Sun in the afternoon when he was high up in the sky.

"Dear friend, do you remember that you

have to return my money?" the Hawk asked the Sun.

The Sun answered, "Yes, I do. But I am in the sky now, and the money is at home. I cannot go home. So please come and meet me when I am at home, and I shall give your money back."

"Sure," said the Hawk.

He decided to meet the Sun the next morning. But the next day, he was late, and the Sun was already in the sky.

The Hawk went to the Sun's house many times, but he never found the Sun there.

Actually, the Sun did not have any money to return to the Hawk. Therefore, he was dodging the Hawk.

One day, on his way to the Sun's house, the Hawk met his friend, the Cock. "Why do you go to the Sun's house every day?" the Cock asked.

The Hawk sadly replied, "I gave him some money a long time ago, and now I cannot get it back! The Sun says he cannot go home to get the money when he is in the

Why do you go to the Sun's house every day?

Stay at my place.

sky. And I can never find him at home. I don't know what to do."

"I can help you," the Cock said. "Come and, stay the night with me at my house. I always get up earlier than the Sun does. I shall wake you up very early. Then you can run quickly to the Sun and get your money."

The Hawk liked the idea. So he stayed with the Cock that night. In the morning the Cock woke up the Hawk. "Cock-a-doodle-doo! Cock-a-doodle-doo! Get up, Hawk! Run to the Sun! He is at home now. He is not up in the sky yet!" the Cock said.

The Hawk got up quickly, thanked the

Poor Hawk, the Sun is fooling him.

Cock and went to the Sun. He knocked at the door. The Sun was still at home. He was sleeping. He wondered who was at his home so early in the morning!

When he opened the door, he was surprised to see the Hawk.

"Good morning, Sun!" said the Hawk, smiling at him. "It is time for you to get up. And I am here to get my money back from you!" "Good morning," said the Sun. "Who told you to come to me so early?"

The Hawk did not answer. The Sun said angrily, "If you want to get your money, you must tell me who told you to come to me so early."

The Hawk answered hesitatingly, "It was

Whose idea was this?

the Cock who told me to see you early in the morning."

The Sun was very angry with the Cock but he pleaded with the Hawk, "Please come tomorrow, I will have your money ready by then. I beg you!" The Hawk was very kind, so he went away.

That night the Hawk stayed with the Cock again.

In the morning, the Cock woke up the Hawk again, "Cock-a-doodle-doo! Get up, Hawk! Run to the Sun!"

However, this time the Sun heard the Cock and ran to the sky, at once. So the Hawk returned empty-handed.

From that day, the Sun always leaves his home whenever the Cock crows to wake up the Hawk.

Moral: Never trust anyone blindly.

The Fire On The Hill

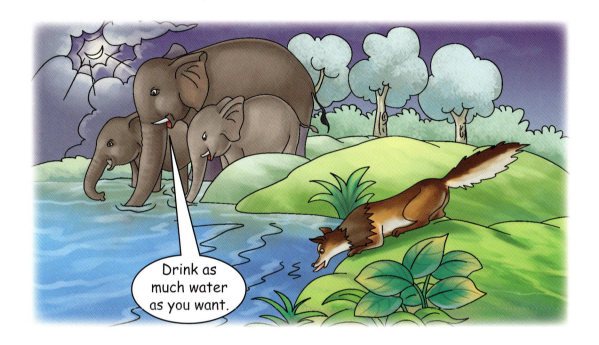

A long time ago, in the Uttarakhand forests, there was a lake of cold water. Many wild animals came to the lake at night to drink water. Thus, the native people never went to the lake at night, fearing that the wild animals would kill and eat them.

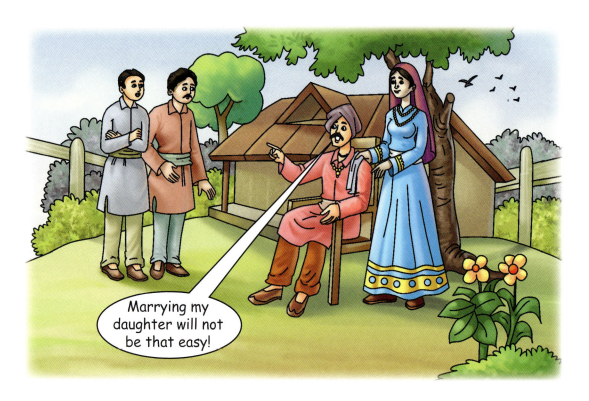

In a village nearby, there lived a rich man who had a beautiful daughter. One day, he declared, "Any young man who will go to the lake and stay in the cold water the entire night, will have my daughter for his wife."

No one in the village wanted to take the risk of staying in the cold water of the lake.

There lived a poor young man in that village who loved the rich man's daughter very much. He said to his mother, "I shall try to stay all night in the lake and then marry the rich man's daughter."

"No, no dear!" the mother cried, "You are my only son! The water in the lake is very cold and the wild animals may eat you

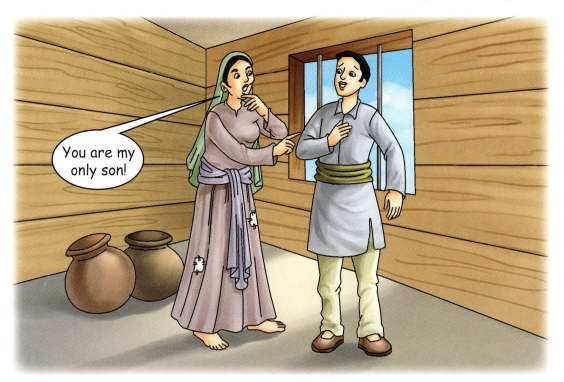

You are my only son!

up. Don't go there! I cannot afford to lose you."

But, the young man did not listen to her. She cried and tried to stop her son. Then her son said, "Mother, don't cry. I must, at least, try to win the challenge. I love the rich man's daughter so much!"

So the young man went to the girl's father.

He told him that he wanted to go to the lake and stay in the cold water all night. The rich man ordered his servants to hide in a place from where they could watch the young man.

When night fell, the young man went to the lake and his mother followed him. But, he did not see her. There was a hill,

Sir, I want to go to the lake.

forty steps away from the place where the young man stood in the water. The young man's mother climbed up the hill and made a fire there. The wild animals saw the fire and were afraid to go near that place.

The young man saw the fire too. He understood that his mother was there. He thought of his mother's love and it was easier for him to stay all night in the cold water.

Then morning came. The young man went to the rich man's house. The rich man saw him and said, "My servants said that there was a fire on a hill, forty steps away from the lake. The fire must

have warmed you and that is why you could stay all night in the water. You have cheated us! So you cannot marry my daughter. Leave now!"

The young man was very angry. He and his mother went to a Judge for justice.

"Well," the Judge said, "this is a very simple case. Come back tomorrow."

The next morning, the young man, his mother and the rich man with his servants went before the Judge.

Soon the hearing of the case began and the Judge asked for a pot of cold water. Then he kept it on the floor and walked forty steps away from it. He made a fire there.

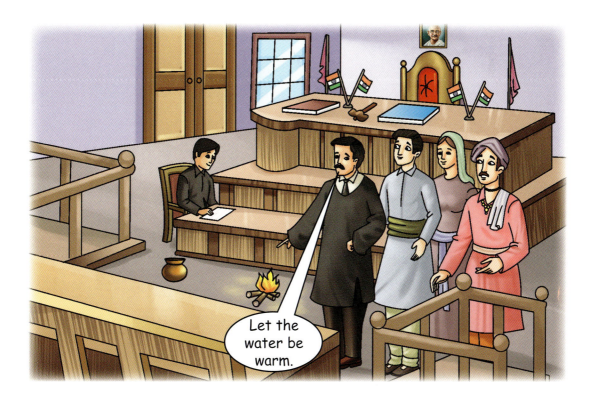

Let the water be warm.

"Now," he said, "we shall wait for a little while until the water is warm."

The people present in the court were surprised at the Judge's act.

The rich man said, "But the fire is far away! How will it warm the water in the pot?"

Then the Judge said, "So, how could that

young man warm himself with a fire that was forty steps away?"

The rich man realised his mistake. He agreed that the young man was very brave to take the risk of staying in the lake's cold water throughout the night. The young man thanked the Judge for rewarding a speedy justice to him.

The young man later married the rich man's daughter. They lived happily for many years.

Moral: Sometimes, common sense comes in handier than the knowledge from books.

The Banyan Tree

In the state of Rajasthan, a tale of a Thakur and a Bania is very popular.

Once upon a time, in a small village of Rajasthan, there lived a Thakur. He had borrowed a large sum of money from a rich Bania. The Bania often asked the Thakur

to repay his money. Despite repeated reminders, the Thakur failed to repay the money.

One day, the Bania went to the Thakur's house when he was sitting with a guest. The Bania demanded his money. The Thakur was very embarrassed. He promised to come to the Bania's place the next day to return the

money. But he had no intention of repaying the loan. Instead, he wanted to take revenge against the Bania for humiliating him in front of his guest.

So that evening, the Thakur stopped the Bania on a deserted stretch. "No one can insult me and get away with it!" he said, drawing out his sword.

I have left a letter with my wife.

The Bania thought quickly and said, "I was expecting you to do something like this. I have left a letter with my wife. If I do not return home by night, she will take the letter to the Village Headman. The letter details the business transaction between us and the steps I took to recover the money. It also expresses the fear that you might harm me."

The Thakur lowered his sword. He knew that the Bania was lying, but he did not want to take a chance. The Village Headman was known to be harsh on defaulters and murderers. Finally, the Thakur said, "I will spare your worthless life, but I will chop off your nose. This will teach you a lesson that you will never forget."

"If I write off your loan, will you forgive me?" asked the Bania.

"I might," the Thakur said guardedly, "but you must give me a receipt that says I have paid you in full, because I don't trust you."

"I will make a receipt right away," said the Bania, hastily opening his bundle of books. "But we will require a witness."

"No witness!" cried the Thakur. "A receipt that says I have repaid your money is enough."

"The receipt has no value unless there is a witness," said the Bania. "Why don't we make that old banyan tree a witness?"

The Thakur reasoned that there could be no harm in making a banyan tree a witness.

Let us make that tree our witness.

It could not reveal the circumstances in which the receipt was made. So, he agreed. They stood under the banyan tree, and the Bania gave the receipt to the Thakur.

The Thakur kept it in his pocket, and went away. He was very pleased with himself. But, the very next day, he received summons from the Village Headman. When he went to the Village Headman's place, he found the Bania there.

"Did you borrow money from this man?" asked the Village Headman.

"I did," answered the Thakur.

"Why haven't you repaid it?"

"I have repaid the money, Sir," said the Thakur. He triumphantly took out the

Sir, I have repaid his loan in full.

receipt from his pocket and handed it over to the Village Headman.

"So your witness was a banyan tree?" asked the Village Headman, looking at the receipt.

"Yes," said the Thakur, "there was no one else there." "So you admit cornering the Bania in a deserted spot?"

"N-No!" stuttered the Thakur. "I...I... just happened to meet him there."

"Anyway this receipt is useless," said the Village Headman. "It does not carry the Bania's signature. It only has the signature of the witness."

"What?" cried the Thakur, taking the paper from the Village Headman's hand.

He stared at it and turned pale. Instead of putting his signature, the Bania had scribbled, 'Banyan Tree.' The Thakur had forgotten to even notice the signatures on the receipt.

The clever Bania had outwitted the Thakur. Thus, the Thakur was duly punished.

Moral: Presence of mind brings great rewards.

The Clever Merchant

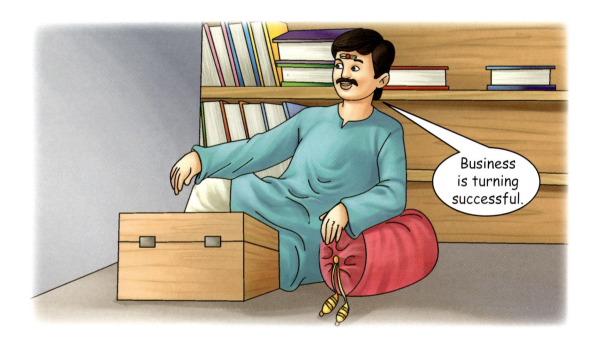

Andhra Pradesh has many interesting folk tales. One of them is that of a clever Merchant and two Goddesses.

Legend has it that the mythological ocean of milk was churned by the gods and demons. They were in search of the divine

nectar that would give them immortality. The radiant and beautiful symbol of prosperity, Goddess Lakshmi, sprung out of this milky ocean. It is said that Jyeshthadevi came out even before Lakshmi, and hence she is considered as the older sister of Lakshmi. When Jyeshthadevi asked the gods what she was supposed to do, she was ordered to dwell in inauspicious places. She is considered to bring sorrow and poverty.

Once, the two sisters Jyeshthadevi, Goddess of poverty, and Lakshmi, Goddess of wealth, had an argument about who was more beautiful and powerful. It was on the occasion of Diwali that the harmless argument started.

Goddess Jyeshthadevi said, "Lakshmi, I am your elder sister, as I was born from the milky ocean much before you. Hence, I am superior to you in every way."

Goddess Lakshmi said, "Sister, I agree that you were born before me, but I am more superior because I am the giver of good fortune and beauty."

Goddess Jyeshthadevi became angry and said, "Don't argue with me! I am much more powerful than you."

Goddess Lakshmi said, "Interestingly, you are a Goddess of misfortune. People believe Lakshmi brings fortunes and Jyeshthadevi brings misfortunes. And people worship both. But, they request

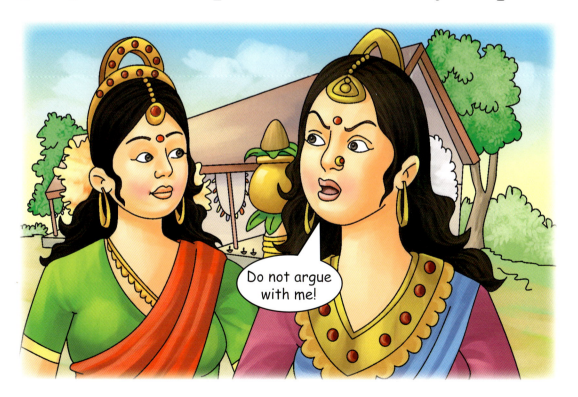

you not to come to their houses."

The fight between the two continued until they both were tired. As the two sisters were arguing, they saw a Merchant coming towards them. They decided to seek his help and settle the matter.

The Merchant was filled with awe when the two sisters told him who they were. They also informed him why they were fighting and asked him to judge who was the most beautiful. The poor Merchant turned pale when he heard their strange request.

It was quite clear to him that Lakshmi was more beautiful of the two. He also knew that Goddess Lakshmi is considered to be the Goddess of wealth, beauty and prosperity.

And that makes her beautiful. But how could he tell Goddess Jyeshthadevi that? She would be furious and would probably reduce him to poverty.

So, the clever Merchant thought of a plan to please both the Goddesses. He told the Goddesses to walk a short distance and then come back to where they had started.

They did what was said and returned.

Quickly gathering his wits, the Merchant said, "Goddess Lakshmi! You are more beautiful than any other woman on earth or in heaven when you are entering a house. It is said that once you leave a home, then violence, frustration, despair and anger rules in it. When you are present in a home,

Please walk a bit.

there is love, peace and prosperity. So you look beautiful while coming in."

Then, he looked at the Goddess Jyeshthadevi and continued, "Goddess, you look beautiful while going out. Words fail to describe your grace and elegance when you are leaving a house. You are at your best while retreating from us. So in common tradition, you are considered the elder sister of Lakshmi. You are also called Alakshmi. On this occasion of Diwali, I would like to invite both of you to visit my house with your respective qualities."

It was a judgement that pleased both the sisters, because each thought she had been adjudged as the winner. But the real winner

of course was the Merchant. He had won
the favour of the Goddess of plenty without
displeasing her powerful rival!

Moral: Always speak the truth in such
a way that no one is hurt.

MEANINGS OF DIFFICULT WORDS

The Fire Festival

Commencement : the beginning; the start

Festivities : celebration of something in a joyful manner

Natural resources : materials such as minerals, forests, water, and fertile land that occur in nature and can be used by people

Survival : to remain alive

Overjoyed : extremely happy

Occasion : a special event or happening

Angrily : feeling or showing anger

Precious : loved or valued very much; rare

The Strangers And The Villagers

Benefit : gain; help; aid

Severely : with sternness; harshly; strictly

Snore	:	to breathe noisily during one's sleep
Supper	:	a meal eaten before going to bed
Stranger	:	a person whom one does not know; an outsider

The Hawk, The Sun And The Cock

Dodging	:	deliberately avoiding; keeping away from
Favour	:	something that you do for someone in order to help them
Hawk	:	a bird of prey, usually with short round wings and a long tail
Hesitatingly	:	to be slow to act, speak, or decide
Plead	:	to ask for something in an urgent or emotional way

The Fire On The Hill

Afford	:	to be able to buy or do something
Declared	:	to make known formally or officially

Handier	: useful; convenient

The Banyan Tree

Cornering	: to force someone into a place that they cannot move away from
Defaulters	: someone who fails to pay money that they owe
Humiliating	: making someone feel ashamed, embarrassed or stupid
Witness	: one who can give a firsthand account of something seen, heard, or experienced
Repay	: to pay back or give back
Deserted	: empty or abandoned area with no people living there
Worthless	: having no value or use
Summons	: a call by an authority to appear, come or do something
Stutter	: to say something with difficulty, repeating the initial consonants of words

The Clever Merchant

Elegance : graceful and attractive in appearance or behaviour

Mythological : relating to a collection of ancient myths, especially those of a particular country or religion

Nectar : the life-giving drink of the gods

Prosperity : the situation of being successful and having a lot of money

Rival : a person who tries to equal or outdo another; competitor

Radiant : shining or glowing brightly

Inauspicious : not favourable; unlucky

Superior : higher in rank, status or quality

Misfortune : bad luck

Furious : very angry; extremely annoyed